Peppa Pig™

Peppa Goes on Holiday

Peppa and her family are going on holiday. Mummy Pig is packing their bags.

"Are you sure we need all that stuff, Mummy Pig?" Daddy Pig asks.
"Yes!" replies Mummy Pig.
"It's all very important!"

Mr Bull takes Peppa, George,
Mummy Pig and Daddy Pig to
the airport in his taxi.

Miss Rabbit checks in their bags.
Then it's time to board the plane.
"Air-plane! Neeeooow!" cries George.

Off they fly, higher and higher through the clouds.

Wheeee!

Before long, their pilot,
Captain Emergency, makes
an announcement:
"We are about to land in Italy."

Miss Rabbit, who is also
their air stewardess, says,
"Please fasten your seat belts."

At the airport in Italy, they collect
their hire car. Once they are on
the road, they discover that the
satnav only speaks Italian!
"Why is everyone beeping their
horns at us?" asks Peppa.
"I expect they are just saying hello,"
says Mummy Pig.

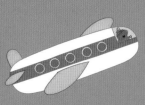

Honk!

Beep!

Beep!

Suddenly Peppa remembers something very important . . . "Teddy! I left Teddy on the aeroplane!"

Oh dear! A policeman on a motorbike pulls Daddy Pig over. "Hello, Officer," stutters Daddy Pig.

"Good day," the policeman replies, reaching into his bag. "I am returning this young bear." "Teddy!" cries Peppa.

Nee-naw!

Nee-naw!

The next day,
Mummy Pig suggests
they do some sightseeing.
Their new friend,
Gabriella Goat, shows
them her pretty village.

Mummy Pig buys a lot of things to take home . . .
They are going to need another suitcase.

Gabriella's uncle shows
Peppa and George
how pizza is made.
"A little bit of
tomato . . . a little
bit of cheese . . ." says
Uncle Goat.

"Into the oven and into
my tummy!" says Peppa.
"I like pizza!"

"What a lovely relaxing holiday!" sighs Mummy Pig, as Daddy Pig drives back to the holiday house.

Oh dear! Daddy Pig has been pulled over again.

"Mr Pig," says the policeman, reaching into his bag. "Your teddy." "Teddy!" cries Peppa.

Nee-naw!
Nee-naw!

After a few days, it is time for
Peppa and her family to go home.
"Bye-bye!" they call to
Gabriella Goat and her family.

"What a lovely holiday," exclaims Daddy Pig. "Yes, I have never felt so relaxed," sighs Mummy Pig.

Oh dear! Daddy Pig has been pulled over by the policeman for a third time!

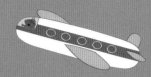

Nee-naw! Nee-naw!

"Mr Pig, please take better care
of your teddy," he says.
"Teddy!" cries Peppa, hugging her
bear. "We're going home today."

Suzy Sheep is waiting for Peppa
when she gets home.

"It rained while you were away,"
Suzy complains.
"Oh good!" cries Peppa. "Holidays
are nice, but coming home to
muddy puddles is even better!"

Collect these other great Peppa Pig stories

Daddy Pig's Office

Dentist Trip

The Story of Prince George

George's First Day at Playgroup

George's New Dinosaur

Peppa Goes Camping

Peppa Goes Skiing

Peppa Goes Swimming

Peppa's First Sleepover

Fun at the Fair

Peppa Meets The Queen

Peppa Pig's Family Computer

George Catches a Cold

Peppa's First Glasses

Peppa Plays Football

George's Balloon